THE ELEMENTAL
PROPHECY

A Fantasy Novel

BY

YASHVIN

The Chronicles of Ipesia:

The Elemental Convergence Series:

The Elemental prophecy

The Wave Walker*

The Embers of Imperium*

The Trials of Time*

The Blood Moon Ascendant*

The Blood Moon Convergence*

Contents

THIS BOOK IS DEDICATED TO

Ms. Sreelatha Kumar

FOREWORD

As the Principal of Junior School at the Aga Khan Academy, Hyderabad, I have close relationships with several of my students, most of whom have been at the Academy since first grade. Yashvin has always been an outstanding student; I have known him for six years. An outspoken, confident student, I remember him mostly for his love for books and reading and his creative and original thoughts and ideas. Therefore, it is no surprise that he has written a novel of such high quality that is so relatable to today's children.

In a world dominated by technology and the onslaught of the unimaginable capabilities of AI, I am certain that books and reading will have an enduring impact on human minds. As a primary school teacher, I firmly believe that language learning is enriched through literature study and even young children benefit from books that use exemplary language and literary elements. Apart from language development, reading literature supports cognitive growth, imagination, emotional understanding, cultural awareness, and meaningful relationships.

Growing up, I remember spending hours in the library reading and borrowing books; however, when I had my children, I read a prolific number of contemporary picture books and young adult fiction. I continue to explore these genres with my grandchildren, which has helped me become a better human being and educator.

By combining fantasy and modern themes, Yashvin has spun a magical yarn that will mesmerize young readers. Reminiscent of well-known books of this genre, 'The Chronicles of Ipesia' has all the characteristics of a best seller, and I'm sure it will make the readers wait anxiously for the sequel. The messages implied in the story are relevant to the world today when we are tackling climate change and the erosion of the Earth's environment. The focus on the elements will bring us literally 'back to earth'! I am immensely proud of Yashvin's achievement.

He is a role model for aspiring young writers and an author who will inspire his peers to read more and write more. My advice to anyone who wishes to write a book: read, read, and then read some more. This will help you to expand your imagination. Next, put your thoughts down on paper and keep writing! I must emphasize here that educators and parents play a pivotal role in nurturing readers and writers. I know Yashvin's parents and how they support and inspire their children to read, learn, and be themselves. Children need independence and agency to act, behave, think, and express themselves to carve their unique identities as individuals.

Ms. Sreelatha Kumar

Principal, Junior School

The Aga Khan Academy, Hyderabad

PREFACE

In the mystical realm of Ipesia, a world steeped in ancient lore and boundless magic, a rare and extraordinary gift is bestowed upon a select few warriors — the ability to wield the essence of existence itself: the elements. From the peaceful flow of water through raging rivers to the dangerous power of time that governs our past, present, and future, these elements hold extraordinary power, capable of reshaping the very fabric of reality.

The elements in Ipesia are not mere occurrences; they are living forces intricately woven into the tapestry of life.

The Wielders

Omega: The Omega are powerful wielders. They can channel more power from the lake of elements than the Alpha. They are the only ones that can control the Difficult Elements. They have a lesser number of people than the Alpha.

Alpha: These Alpha have higher numbers of people than that of the Omega. They can channel slightly fewer powers, and very few have been known to control the difficult elements. The most famous of these beings is the legendary Shadow knight.

BASIC ELEMENTS

Water: Masters of water manipulation can control all forms of liquids, with the Omega among them transmuting liquids into solid states. Aiden Navvaro(Alpha) is a Water manipulator.

Fire: Fire wielders harness the destructive force of fire. Some elite Alphas conjure blue flames, known as the Alpha Holocaust, while all Omegas wield Hell-fire, also known as Omega Inferno. Reka Almanara(Alpha) is a Fire wielder.

Wind: Wind, considered the most delicate of the basic elements, allows users to survive falls from any height, and many can travel vast distances in the blink of an eye.

Earth: The least common of the basic elements, mastering earth requires a lot of skill. Once mastered, it becomes an important tool for defense, offense, and even serves as a healing element in times of war.

DIFFICULT ELEMENTS

Mind: Those with control over the mind have telepathic and telekinetic abilities. Advanced Alphas can search for DNA signatures across the world, while Omegas can achieve teleportation of both themselves and objects.

Digital: Manipulators of the digital realm are talented at conjuring futuristic gadgets, vehicles, and even entire towns within moments.

Darkness: The most perilous of elements, unchained darkness threatens the very existence of Ipesia. Only the Omega possesses the formidable power to channel and control it. Kael Baudelaire (Omega) is a Shadow weaver.

Light: The element of the purest Omega, light not only shields allies from elemental attacks but also becomes a healing force in the hands of advanced users, making them invaluable medics.

Time: A complex, important element, time manipulators can peer into many possible outcomes of their actions, traverse both backward and forward in time, alter timelines, and crucially manipulate their own and others' ages. Zara Avivi(Omega) is a time controller.

Prologue

The sun had cast its golden glow upon the small village on the outskirts of the Water City. Much like any other, it was a peaceful morning as the villagers went around doing their daily activities. In a cozy cottage decorated with detailed seashell decorations, a loving family prepared for a wonderful day that would change young Aiden's life forever.

With his inquisitive sea-green eyes reflecting the crystal-clear waters of his homeland, Aiden stood at the center of the cottage's cozy living room. His parents, Clara and Lucas, warmly smiled as they approached him. Aiden's heart raced with excitement; he could hardly believe the day had finally come. Today, he was told that he would be given a precious gift - a gift that held the power of his ancestors, a gift that would connect him to the original elemental forces of Ipesia.

Clara held her delicate hands, a glimmering blue crystal nestled in the center of her palms. It's aquamarine and deep blue hues pulsated with a gentle light, casting colorful reflections on the walls. "Aiden, my love," she said softly, "this crystal is a part of who we are, a gift from our ancestors. With it, you can connect to the water's essence better than anyone."

Lucas joined them, his voice filled with pride. "Your mother and I have always known you're destined for greatness, Aiden. This crystal will guide you in that path."

Aiden's heart swelled with gratitude and excitement. He took the crystal in his small hands, feeling its energy pulsate with his very being. The air seemed to shimmer with excitement as if nature itself recognized this important moment.

Aiden's parents shared stories of their journeys as the sun dipped below the horizon. The room was bathed in a warm, amber glow as the hearth crackled with fire, casting jumping shadows on the walls.

~~~

As the following day dawned, casting golden light across the village and into the cottage where Aiden and his parents lived. A gentle breeze whispered through the open windows, carrying the scent of the sea, but as the day continued, a dark cloud gathered on the horizon.

A knock echoed through the cottage. Clara's smile wavered, and Lucas's brow furrowed with concern. The village was a haven of peace, untouched by the chaos that lay beyond its borders. Who would want to find them with so much urgency?
~~~

Aiden watched as his parents exchanged tense glances before opening the door. And there, in their doorway, stood a figure clouded in darkness, its features blocked by a cloak that seemed to absorb the very light around it.

"Give it to me," the figure's voice was an unsettling whisper, the words dripping with a creepy authority. "I shall possess it one way or the other. "

Aiden's heart raced, his grip on his crystal tightening involuntarily. Fear gripped his chest, and he stepped back, his gaze darting between the figure and his parents.

Clara and Lucas exchanged a knowing look, their expressions filled with a mixture of determination and sorrow. "You cannot have it," Clara's voice trembled, but the opposition in her voice was clear. "Our son's destiny lies with this crystal. We will not surrender it to darkness."

The figure's laughter was a haunting melody that echoed through the room. "Stubborn fools," it hissed. "You cannot escape your fate nor protect him forever."

The figure shot a dart of darkness in an instant, and Lucas countered it with a water shield. The house had become a battleground of powerful forces. Water clashed with shadows, a dance of power that shook the foundation of the cottage. Aiden watched in horror as his parents fought valiantly, their forms surrounded by torrents of water as they defended against the violent darkness.

But the figure's power was unlike anything they had ever faced. It seemed to gather energy with their efforts, and despite their strength, they were pushed to the brink of exhaustion within seconds. With a final surge, the figure's outstretched hand sent a wave of darkness crashing over Clara and Lucas. Aiden's world shattered at that moment. Time seemed to stretch, his vision narrowing involuntarily to the sight of his parents falling to the ground, their forms lifeless and broken. Suddenly, a wave of nausea and dizziness crept over him, and he fell. As he fell, he saw the crystal in his hand burst with an aquamarine glow, blinding him...

I

<u>CHAPTER 1: SHADOWS OF IAKRUS</u>

The morning sun bathed Iakrus in a warm, golden light as Aiden made his way through its bustling streets. Tall stone and glass buildings towered above, casting long shadows on the cobbled paths below. The aroma of street vendors' delicacies filled the air, tempting passersby with breakfast delights. Iakrus was unlike any other city, where magic and wonder were woven into everyday life.

Aiden walked with purpose, his leather satchel containing his textbooks and scrolls slung over his shoulder. He greeted familiar faces and exchanged morning pleasantries with merchants setting up their stalls. Iakrus wasn't just his home; it was where he had grown and flourished, surrounded by enchantment and beauty.

Approaching the grand gates of the Iakrus Academy, Aiden beheld the imposing stone structure before him. It was a place of wonder and challenge, where knowledge and mastery of magic were paramount. Since childhood, he had dreamt of attending this prestigious institution, and now he stood on the threshold of his dreams.

Reka, his closest friend since their arrival at the Academy, joined him on the path. Her emerald eyes sparkled with curiosity and determination, her fiery red hair catching the morning light.

"Aiden," she said, "you seem preoccupied this morning. Is something troubling you?"

Aiden hesitated, then sighed. "It's a strange dream, Reka— the first time I've had it. It was about a burning forest and a mysterious figure."

Reka's expression softened, and she placed a reassuring hand on his arm. "You should speak to Master Elara about it. She might have some insights."

Master Elara, his water element trainer, had been guiding him since his arrival at the Academy. She had recognized his potential as a water manipulator and had been instrumental in his growth.

Aiden nodded, grateful for her understanding. "I think I will, Reka."

~~~

The halls of the Academy buzzed with activity as students hurried to their morning lectures. Aiden and Reka attended classes on elemental magic, history, and combat, each lesson a stepping stone on their path to becoming skilled mages.

During his elemental training class, Aiden struggled to control the water element. While his classmates effortlessly conjured flames and summoned gusts of wind, his attempts yielded little more than a few errant droplets.

Master Elara observed him closely, her perceptive eyes narrowing with concern. The training room, with its large arched windows and crystal-clear water pool, provided a serene backdrop for their practice. Aiden's classmates gathered around, curious to see how he would fare.

However, today was different for Aiden. The vivid dream from the previous night lingered in his mind like a haunting
~~~

specter, disrupting his concentration and unsettling his thoughts.

Master Elara noticed his struggle and stepped forward. "Aiden, clear your mind. Focus on the water within you."

Aiden nodded, attempting to shake off the disquieting memories. He closed his eyes, taking a deep breath to center himself. As he regained control, the water responded more obediently to his commands.

The classmates watched in awe as Aiden's control improved, transforming the erratic droplets into graceful arcs. Master Elara nodded approvingly, acknowledging the effort it took for him to regain control.

~~~

As evening descended upon Iakrus, Aiden, and Reka sat by the serene canal that wound through the city. They talked about their past years at the Academy, their voices filled with warmth and laughter.

Suddenly, a bone-chilling cold descended upon Aiden's shoulder, causing him to shiver. He turned, expecting to see someone behind him, but no one was there. Reka looked around in confusion.
~~~

"What's wrong?" she asked, noticing his unease.

Aiden whispered, his breath visible in the frigid air. "I felt... a cold hand on my shoulder."

A mischievous voice echoed from behind them, breaking the stillness of the evening. "BOO!"

Chapter 2: The Call Of Whispered Secrets

The tranquil embrace of the canal cradled Aiden as he emerged, water dripping from his clothes, surprise etched across his face like an ephemeral painting in the twilight. Laughter, like a lively symphony, bubbled forth, echoing through the air as the orchestrator of this watery surprise revealed himself – Kael, the shadow-weaver. With her emerald eyes reflecting the amusement within, Zara seamlessly joined the laughter. The prank had unfolded with a choreography only they understood, and the ripples of mirth echoed across the canal's surface, creating a dance of shimmering reflections. Aiden, though initially startled, soon became a willing participant in the laughter, acknowledging the well-executed surprise with a grin that mirrored the sparkle in Zara's eyes.

As the laughter subsided, Reka, their trusted friend and accomplice, stepped forward with an arched eyebrow. "Late again, you two? What grand scheme were you hatching this time?"

Zara and Kael exchanged knowing glances, their laughter turning mischievous. Zara stepped forward, a playful smile playing on her lips. "Reka, my dear, we were fashionably late because we were perfecting the art of surprise. Every great entrance needs meticulous planning."

Reka, though scolding, couldn't suppress a smile, appreciating the gleam of mischief in her friends' eyes. "Meticulous planning, huh? I hope your grand entrance was worth the wait."

Zara nodded, her eyes sparkling with untamed joy. "Oh, it absolutely was. We had to consider all possible outcomes and the steps to follow to make it perfect. It's an art, really."

Reka sighed in mock exasperation, shaking her head in a blend of fondness and amusement. "You two and your antics. Let's get back before we turn this canal into a stage for more mischief."

Just as they turned to leave, Aiden, the master of water manipulation, couldn't resist adding his own playful twist to the scene. Zara watched with amusement as he flicked his wrist, summoning a stream of water from the canal. It cascaded towards the trio, a watery dance that added a refreshing touch to the warm evening.

Laughter erupted once more, blending with the soothing sounds of flowing water. Zara couldn't help but admire Aiden's mastery of the elements, a reminder of the unique talents each of them brought to their group. The camaraderie among them was as fluid as the water Aiden commanded, weaving a tapestry of shared laughter and unspoken bonds against the canvas of the tranquil canal.

~~~

The group made their way to the lavish apartments allocated to them. The pathway split, leading Reka and Zara to the upper floor while Aiden and Kael proceeded to the lower floor. The magical apartments were a testament to the Academy's
~~~

grandeur, nestled amidst lush gardens and adorned with intricate magical symbols.

As Reka and Zara approached their floor, the intricate designs on the façade glowed in response to their presence, and the ornate door swung open in a silent welcome. The interior was as enchanting as the exterior, with spacious rooms and an ethereal ambiance that whispered of magical craftsmanship.

Meanwhile, Aiden and Kael walked toward their designated apartment on the lower floor. They exchanged casual banter about the day's events, discussing plans for the upcoming magical combat training. Upon reaching their apartment, they decided to freshen up before joining the girls on the upper floor.

Unknown to them, Reka and Zara had planned a night of games and relaxation. Plush couches and vibrant tapestries adorned the living room, creating a cozy setting for their evening together. The anticipation of shared laughter and camaraderie lingered in the air.

Aiden and Kael, now clad in comfortable attire, ascended to the upper floor to join the girls. The girls welcomed them with smiles, and the group settled into the inviting atmosphere of the living room. Together, they enjoyed and played board games.

Zara and Reka destroyed the boys at all the games. Then Zara remembered something. She decided to tell Reka.

Just as Zara opened her mouth to share the disturbing glimpse of the future she had witnessed, they reached the entrance of their villa. Aiden and Kael exchanged knowing glances, aware of the unspoken connection between the two girls but respecting the need for privacy.

"Save that thought for later," Reka said with a playful wink, unlocking the door to their villa. "We wouldn't want to spoil the evening."

Zara nodded, a hint of reluctance in her eyes. "You're right. Later, then."

Aiden and Kael exchanged knowing glances, aware of the unspoken connection between the two girls but respecting the need for privacy.

As the girls suddenly quietened, Aiden turned to Kael with a smirk. "What do you think they're talking about?"

Kael shrugged, his eyes gleaming with mischief. "Probably world domination. Girls and their secrets, you know."

In the midst of their conversation, Zara felt an unexpected wave of dizziness. The world around her seemed to sway, and she staggered, narrowly missing the edge of the plush couch. Reka, engrossed in their conversation, didn't notice the near-miss.

On the other hand, Aiden couldn't help but observe Zara's unsteady stance. "You okay there, Zara?"

Zara, trying to play it cool, flashed a quick grin. "Just a bit dizzy. Must be the excitement of the day catching up to me."

As she excused herself and headed to her room, she stumbled once more, and with a comedic twist of fate, she missed the bed by mere inches. Suppressing a chuckle, Aiden couldn't resist a playful comment, "I guess mastering the art of surprise comes with its own surprises."

"Shut up, Navvaro" retorted Zara.

Zara knew that Aiden would make a witty remark, but it never came. She looked over to Aiden, but he seemed a little distracted and looked down at his crystal, which hung around his neck at all times. Zara then realized that his surname reminded him of his parents, who had passed away long ago. Aiden never shared the details of what happened to his parents, but Zara, Reka, and Kael understood that the crystal was the last reminder of his parents.

Soon, Zara drifted off to sleep, looking at the everchanging design of the roof.

~~~

The corridors of the Iakrus Academy buzzed with the vibrant energy of students heading to their morning classes. Zara and Reka navigated the familiar pathways, their footsteps echoing against the polished stone floors. As they approached the grand entrance of the Academy, the towering doors swung open, welcoming them into the heart of magical learning.

The Academy's majestic halls were adorned with intricate tapestries and adorned with symbols of elemental mastery. Students of various talents and backgrounds bustled about, their conversations weaving into a harmonious symphony of knowledge and camaraderie.

Zara and Reka made their way to the elemental lore class, where Master Seraphina, a wise and ancient sorceress, delved into the intricacies of the magical realms. The walls of the classroom were adorned with artifacts and relics, each holding a story of ancient enchantments and forgotten legends.

As the class progressed, Master Seraphina spoke of the mystical places hidden within Ipesia—secret realms where the veil between dimensions was thin, allowing for glimpses of
~~~

otherworldly wonders. The mention of the Whispering Grove, a place where the trees carried the echoes of ancient prophecies, piqued Zara's curiosity.

<div align="center">~~~</div>

After the class, Zara and Reka found themselves drawn to the notion of exploring one of these mystical places. As they exited the classroom, Reka turned to Zara with a mischievous gleam in her eyes.

"Whispering Grove, what do you say? A little detour from our usual routine?"

"No, Reka. It's outside the city limits," said Zara. "We'll probably get that route on our element race."

"Ok then, let's go tell the boys about the Whispering Grove," Reka said reluctantly.

"Race you to the Combat Arena." Said Zara, running off.

The Combat Arena stood as a testament to the prowess of Iakrus Academy's most skilled elemental wielders. Massive stone pillars surrounded a central battleground where students honed their combat skills. The echoes of clashing elements and the occasional roar of summoned creatures filled the air.

Zara and Reka reached the arena, their breaths slightly hurried from the playful race. They found a spot to watch the ongoing training sessions, leaning against the stone railing that overlooked the battleground. The energy within the arena was palpable, a fusion of magical prowess and competitive spirit.

As they waited for Aiden and Kael to finish their combat training, the arena erupted in a display of unparalleled elemental mastery. With his water manipulation, Aiden created intricate shapes and sculptures that danced in harmony with Kael's swirling shadows. The audience, a mix of admiration and awe, watched as the two friends seamlessly blended their elemental forces.

Aiden summoned cascading waterfalls that twisted into serpentine forms while Kael's shadows wove around them like ethereal dancers. The combination of water and shadows created a mesmerizing spectacle, leaving spectators entranced by the fluidity of their movements.

Reka nudged Zara, her eyes reflecting the amazement of the spectacle before them. "Look at them go. Aiden and Kael truly are the best elemental controllers in the Academy."

Zara nodded, her gaze fixed on the arena. "Their coordination is unparalleled. It's like they share a connection beyond just friendship."

As the combat session reached its climax, Aiden and Kael executed a synchronized move that sent ripples through the arena. A surge of water entwined with shadows surged forward, creating a breathtaking display of elemental power. The crowd erupted in cheers, acknowledging the mastery of the two friends.

After the training session concluded, Aiden and Kael approached Zara and Reka, their expressions a mix of exhaustion and satisfaction.

"Quite the performance, wouldn't you say?" Aiden grinned, beads of water still glistening on his fingertips.

Kael, the shadow-weaver, added with a smirk, "No one can match the elegance of water and shadows combined."

Reka chuckled, "You both never cease to amaze. We were thinking of telling you about something interesting we heard in class..."

III

CHAPTER 3: TIDES OF TIME

Kael surveyed the arena, its pulsating energy of magic and camaraderie swirling around him. Zara and Reka leaned against the stone railing, their eyes fixed on the ongoing spectacle below. He couldn't help but feel a sense of pride as the whispers of admiration filled the air.

As Aiden and he continued their elemental display, Kael reveled in the harmony of water and shadows. The fluid movements of cascading waterfalls intertwined with the elusive dance of shadows, creating a tapestry of magic that captivated the audience. The cheers and gasps of onlookers fueled the fire of his elemental prowess.

Glancing toward the stands, expecting to see Master Shimazu, the teacher of elemental combat and physical combat, Kael was surprised to see Reka and Zara looking down, flashing a thumbs-up sign. Kael smirked, embracing the acknowledgment. As the combat session reached its zenith, a synchronized display of water and shadows erupted, earning them thunderous applause. Aiden's water is entwined with Kael's shadows, creating a breathtaking fusion of elegance and power.

After the training session, Aiden and Kael approached Zara and Reka, beads of water still glistening on Aiden's fingertips. Aiden grinned, "Quite the performance, wouldn't you say?"

Kael added his own touch of mischief, "No one can match the elegance of water and shadows combined."

Reka chuckled, her laughter echoing in the aftermath of their elemental display. "You both never cease to amaze. We were thinking of telling you about something interesting we heard in class."

Zara's eyes glowed with a sudden realization. "Actually, I was thinking of showing you..."

~~~

In the blink of an eye, the surroundings shifted, and the familiar sights of the Combat Arena were replaced by a swirling vortex of ethereal lights. The air crackled with magical energy as random events unfolded around them, snippets of moments just before the girls reached the arena. Laughter, elemental displays, and snippets of conversations intertwined in the chaotic dance of the vortex.

Abruptly, the vortex faded away, leaving them standing outside Master Seraphina's class. Zara, her eyes shimmering with the residue of time magic, took a step forward, and her voice carried a tone of urgency. "Listen carefully, everyone. I just took us back in time, and our past selves are in that class. We can't let them see us; it would cause a feedback loop and intense headaches. Stay alert."

Reka and Zara exchanged knowing glances, a silent understanding passing between them. As the class progressed, Master Seraphina delved into the mysteries of the mystical realms within Ipesia, mentioning the Whispering Grove—a
~~~

place where ancient prophecies echoed through the rustling leaves.

After the class concluded, Zara and Reka guided the group away from the past versions of themselves. As they walked, other versions of Reka and Zara emerged from the classroom. The air shimmered with a surreal quality as two sets of the same individuals coexisted.

Reka's past self turned to Zara with a mischievous gleam. "Whispering Grove, what do you say? A little detour from our usual routine?"

"No, Reka. It's outside the city limits," past Zara replied. "We'll probably get that route on our element race."

Reka's past self sighed in reluctant agreement. "Okay then, let's go tell the boys about the Whispering Grove." With a playful challenge, she added, "Race you to the Combat Arena."

Past Zara wasted no time, dashing off with a mischievous glint in her eyes. The present group exchanged amused glances, silently witnessing the echo of a moment that had already played out. The timeline was intact.

Once the group recovered from the shock of what they had just seen, Aiden couldn't contain his curiosity. "This is incredible, Zara, but how do we get back to our timeline?"

With a mischievous glint in her eye, Zara teased, "Well, maybe you're stuck here forever. Welcome to the past!"

The boys exchanged amused glances, but a hint of concern flickered in their eyes. Zara couldn't keep up the act for long, and with a burst of laughter, she reassured them, "Just kidding! Hold hands, everyone. We're going back."

The group formed a circle, hands clasped together. Zara focused her magic, and once again, the vortex of lights enveloped them. Time twisted and turned as they journeyed back to the present.

Aiden, Kael, and Reka looked around in amazement as they emerged from the temporal vortex. The transition from one timeline to another had been a surreal experience, leaving them with a sense of wonder.

"Did you see that?" Aiden exclaimed, his eyes wide with astonishment.

Kael, usually composed, couldn't hide his excitement. "That was like riding the currents of time itself."

With a grin, Reka added, "Zara, you sure know how to make time travel an adventure."

Zara, pleased with their reactions, chuckled. "Well, time travel is all in good fun, but we're back in the present now. Let's focus on it rather than dwell on past events."

Kael observed the group, still buzzing with the lingering excitement of their temporal journey.

As they ventured forward, Kael noticed a subtle change in Zara's demeanor. Her laughter ceased, and a fleeting shadow crossed her features. He furrowed his brow, concern flickering in his eyes. "Zara, are you alright?"

Zara, attempting to dismiss the unease, forced a smile. "I'm fine, just a bit dizzy from the time-traveling escapade. It's nothing."

The group continued walking, but Kael kept a watchful eye on Zara. Suddenly, her steps faltered, and she swayed, a sudden pallor washing over her face. Before anyone could react, Zara's eyes rolled back, and she collapsed, unconscious.

~~~

The infirmary exuded an air of hushed concern as Kael paced back and forth, his footsteps echoing off the sterile walls. Zara
~~~

lay on the healing bed, her form still and serene, contrasting sharply with the undercurrent of tension in the room. The healer, a figure cloaked in robes adorned with mystical symbols, moved with practiced grace, their hands emitting a soft glow as they attended Zara.

Every tick of the clock felt like an eternity, each moment stretching as Kael anxiously awaited any sign of improvement. With a reassuring nod, the healer finally spoke, "It appears to be exhaustion, a consequence of the strain from time-traveling. She will recover, but rest is crucial."

A collective sigh of relief seemed to fill the room as Zara stirred after what felt like an eternity. Her emerald eyes slowly opened, adjusting to the soft light of the infirmary. Kael approached her bedside, concern, and relief evident in his voice. "Zara, are you okay?"

Groggily, Zara nodded, her gaze flitting around the room as she tried to make sense of her surroundings. "Yeah, just a bit drained. What happened?"

"You fainted," Aiden explained, his worry palpable. "We brought you to the infirmary. How are you feeling now?"

A weak but genuine smile graced Zara's lips. "I'll survive. Thanks for looking out for me, guys."

Reka grinned. "Well, you better because we've got a special assembly to attend. The Grandmaster has arranged something, and it's in three hours. You should rest up."

After discharging Zara from the infirmary and walking out, the group found themselves bathed in the soft glow of the Academy's magical lights. Zara's steps became more assured, her vitality gradually returning. The cadence of their laughter echoed through the corridors as they made their way toward the grand entrance.

As they stepped out of the infirmary, the air seemed to carry a lighter energy. Zara walked with a bit more spring in her step, and the effects of rest were evident in her demeanor. The group strolled through the Academy's corridors, the echo of their footsteps accompanying the murmur of conversation.

Kael couldn't help but glance at Zara, concern lingering in his eyes. "You sure you're up for this, Zara?"

She shot him a reassuring grin. "Absolutely. I've napped away whatever time-travel fatigue I had. Let's focus on what the Grandmaster has in store for us."

Ever the optimistic spirit, Reka interjected, "I bet it's something exciting. Maybe a magical tournament or an inter-elemental challenge!"

Aiden, who had been mostly quiet, added, "Whatever it is, we'll face it together. That's what we've always done."

As they approached the entrance of the infirmary, Zara playfully nudged Kael. "Hey, Kael, any ideas on what the Grandmaster might announce?"

Aiden, thoughtful as always, chimed in, "I've heard rumors about an artifact hidden within the Academy. Maybe he'll announce a quest to find it."

Zara, back to her mischievous self, couldn't resist teasing. "Aiden, you and your artifacts. Are you sure it's not just a lost sock?"

Aiden grinned, "Lost artifacts, lost socks—both equally mysterious."

Kael grinned, his eyes gleaming with mischief. "Maybe a surprise test on controlling shadowy serpents and watery illusions?"

Zara mock gasped, "You're not giving him ideas, are you?"

Reka laughed, "I, for one, am ready for anything. Bring it on, Grandmaster!"

They continued bantering and speculating, their voices weaving a tapestry of camaraderie. The Academy's surroundings seemed to respond to their infectious energy, magical symbols glowing brighter in acknowledgment.

Upon reaching the grand entrance of the assembly hall, Kael looked at Zara with a playful challenge. "Ready to face the unknown, time-traveler?"

Zara rolled her eyes, but the sparkle in them revealed her playful spirit. "Always. Let's see what awaits us."

As they waited for the doors to open, the anticipation in the air was palpable, a shared excitement binding the group together. Whatever lay ahead, they were prepared to face it as a team, united by the magic that wove their destinies together.

IV

CHAPTER 4: THE ANNOUNCEMENT

The Grandmaster Guadalupe stood at the podium, her presence commanding the attention of every student in the assembly hall. The vast space buzzed with magical energy as the students awaited the announcement that hung in the air.

"As we embark on a new phase of learning and growth," Grandmaster Guadalupe's voice resonated, "it is time for a challenge that will test your elemental mastery, teamwork, and resilience. The journey of a magician extends beyond the confines of textbooks and classrooms. It is in the real-world application of your abilities that you truly discover your potential."

Reka's excitement surged as the Grandmaster continued, introducing the pivotal components of the challenge. "We shall have an Elemental Race and Combat. This will not be a conventional exam but a combination of combat and wilderness race. You will face challenges that will require not only your mastery of elements but also your ability to navigate the untamed wilderness. It is in adversity that one truly learns the extent of their capabilities."

The notion of combining their elemental prowess with the strategic demands of the wilderness ignited a spark within Reka. The untamed wilderness became an arena for them to showcase not only their magical skills but also their ability to adapt and overcome unforeseen obstacles.

Grandmaster Guadalupe's words took a more specific turn as she delved into the combat aspect of the challenge. "You will be grouped into teams of four, and each team will navigate a course designed to test your elemental skills and strategic thinking. The race will take you through enchanted forests, rushing rivers, and mysterious caverns. Along the way, you will encounter both magical creatures and elemental obstacles, each a testament to the unpredictability of the magical realms."

The mention of magical creatures and elemental obstacles added a layer of complexity to the challenge. Reka's mind raced with the possibilities, contemplating the kind of adversaries they might encounter. The prospect of real combat, where their skills would be put to the test against both nature and magical beings, was both exhilarating and daunting.

As the Grandmaster continued, Reka couldn't help but glance at her friends—Zara, Aiden, and Kael. Their eyes held a shared determination, a silent agreement that they were ready to face whatever challenges awaited them.

"Prepare yourselves," the Grandmaster advised, her gaze encompassing the entire assembly. "The Elemental Race and Combat will begin in two days. Use this time to strategize, refine your skills, and embrace the unity of your elemental talents. Remember, it is not just a race against time, but a journey of self-discovery and camaraderie."

Reka's mind buzzed with excitement and a touch of nervousness. The combination of elemental mastery, wilderness navigation, and real combat presented a multifaceted challenge that promised growth and adventure. The revealed route, a critical piece of the puzzle, would be disclosed two days from now, leaving them with anticipation and a sense of urgency. As the assembly dispersed, discussions among the students filled the air.

~~~

As the excitement lingered in the air, a figure approached the group, a sly grin etched across his face. It was Marcus, a known troublemaker, a self-proclaimed expert in elemental combat, and a master of the element Earth. His eyes, filled with arrogance, shifted toward Aiden, Kael, Zara, and Reka.

"Well, well, well," Marcus sneered, "if it isn't the squad of misfits gearing up for the Elemental Race and Combat. News travels fast in this Academy, you know."

Aiden, Kael, Zara, and Reka exchanged glances, their expressions a mix of irritation and indifference. Marcus had a reputation for being a bully, especially when it came to flaunting his skills in elemental manipulation.

Marcus focused his attention on Aiden, smirking condescendingly. "You might want to save yourself some embarrassment, Water-boy. The race requires more than just splashing around with your little water tricks."

Aiden maintained his composure, choosing not to be drawn into Marcus's provocation. "We'll see how things unfold,
~~~

Marcus. It's not just about the elements; it's about strategy and teamwork."

Marcus chuckled dismissively, then turned his gaze to Kael. "And you, with your shadowy illusions. Shadows won't save you in the wild, my friend. This is not one of your bedtime stories."

Kael, unfazed, responded with a calm demeanor, "We'll let our actions speak for us, Marcus."

Reka, unable to resist a retort, added, "And you might want to focus on your own team. We've got our own plans."

Marcus leaned in, his voice dripping with arrogance, addressing the boys specifically, "Just a piece of advice, losers: stay out of our way. You might end up getting hurt trying to keep up with the best."

As Marcus walked away, his laughter echoed in the corridor. While irritated by his arrogance, the trio chose to brush off the encounter. Aiden glanced at Kael and Reka, a determined glint in his eyes. "Let's prove him wrong together."

Kael nodded, a smirk playing on his lips. "Absolutely. We've faced tougher challenges than him."

Zara, ever the optimist, added, "And we've always come out on top. Let's focus on our strategy and training. Marcus is just noise in the background."

With renewed determination, the trio walked away from the encounter, ready to face the upcoming challenge with resilience and unity. The looming Elemental Race and Combat held the promise of not only testing their magical abilities but also proving the strength of their bonds against those who sought to belittle them.

~~~

The Combat Arena buzzed with heightened energy as students from various elemental disciplines gathered for intensive practice sessions. The cancellation of regular classes allowed them ample time to refine their skills, strategize with their teams, and prepare for the upcoming Elemental Race and Combat.

Reka, Zara, Aiden, and Kael engaged in a series of collaborative exercises, testing their coordination and elemental synergy. The sun dipped low on the horizon as they honed their combat techniques, the echoes of elemental clashes filling the arena.
~~~

As the group took a moment to catch their breath, Master Shimazu, a seasoned instructor known for his stern yet effective teaching methods, approached them. "Your teamwork shows promise, but there's always room for improvement. I've arranged a practice battle between your team and Marcus' group."

Reka exchanged a glance with her friends, the challenge sparking a fire in their eyes. Marcus, the overconfident troublemaker, led a team with an eclectic mix of elemental abilities—earth, wind, digital, and mind. It was a clash of elements and egos.

Marcus, a burly figure with an air of arrogance, commanded the earth, summoning stone barriers and launching boulders with a menacing grin. Beside him, Skylar, a swift and agile wind wielder, danced through the air, creating whirlwinds that twisted and turned unpredictably.

On the digital front, Alex, a tech-savvy mage, manipulated illusions and holographic projections, creating a maze of confusion for the opponents. Meanwhile, Evelyn, a master of mind manipulation, delved into the thoughts and emotions of her adversaries, seeking weaknesses to exploit.

The Combat Arena transformed into a battleground of magic, each student a master of their respective elements. Aiden conjured waterfalls that twisted and danced, Kael's shadows swirled like mischievous spirits, Zara wielded fire with an almost playful grace, and Reka harnessed the wind to maneuver with unparalleled agility.

Marcus' crew responded with a calculated dance of earth, wind, digital illusions, and mind-bending projections. Skylar's winds clashed with Aiden's water, creating a spectacle of mist and gusts. Alex's digital illusions intertwined with Kael's shadows, casting ethereal landscapes upon the arena.

In the mental realm, Evelyn engaged in a subtle dance with Zara, probing the depths of the fiery mage's thoughts while Zara resisted with a determined focus. The arena crackled with energy as clashes of elements painted a vivid tapestry in the air.

In the midst of the chaos, Reka felt a surge of determination. Marcus' taunts fueled a fiery resolve within her, and the seamless cooperation with her friends created a symphony of power that transcended individual abilities.

As the final elemental clashes echoed through the arena, Master Shimazu stepped forward, his eyes gleaming with wisdom. "Well-fought, both teams. Remember, the key lies not just in mastering your element but in the synergy between you and your comrades."

With the practice battle concluded, Reka and her friends left the Combat Arena, their spirits soaring. The lessons learned in the crucible of elemental combat were more than just skills; they were bonds forged in the fires of teamwork and resilience. The looming Elemental Race and Combat suddenly felt like an epic quest, and with newfound insights and camaraderie, they were ready to face whatever challenges the magical world had in store for them.

The practice battle left an electric energy in the air, a sense of accomplishment mingled with anticipation. As Reka and her friends exited the Combat Arena, the setting sun casting hues of orange and pink, they headed toward the locker rooms to debrief and prepare for the Elemental Race and Combat that loomed ahead.

Inside the locker room, Marcus couldn't resist the opportunity to gloat. "Well, well, well. Seems like my team went easy on you guys. Didn't want to bruise your egos too much, you know?"

Reka rolled her eyes, unimpressed by Marcus' posturing. "Sure, Marcus. Your team was practically holding back hurricanes and earthquakes."

Kael, never one to shy away from a challenge, decided to have a bit of fun. He stepped forward, his eyes narrowing as he conjured a swirling mass of shadows around Marcus. The boastful bully scoffed, "What's this supposed to be, Kael? Trying to scare me with your shadow puppets?"

Before Kael could respond, Evelyn, the mind manipulator from Marcus' team, calmly intervened. With a subtle gesture, she dispelled the dark illusion, her eyes locking onto Kael's. "Nice try, shadow-boy. Mind games won't work on us."

The exchange added fuel to the rivalry between the two teams. Marcus, convinced of his superiority, continued to taunt and boast, while Kael maintained a stoic demeanor, a glint of determination in his eyes. Kael was getting mad.

Kael conjured the swirling shadows; he focused his intent, weaving the illusion to tap into Marcus' deepest fears. The shadows enveloped Marcus, and for a moment, the locker room disappeared, replaced by a nightmarish landscape that mirrored the darkest corners of Marcus' mind.

Haunted by his worst fears, Marcus found himself trapped in a labyrinth of shadows, where echoes of his insecurities and anxieties manifested as sinister specters. The illusion was a dance of horrors, a vivid reflection of the fears he concealed beneath his arrogant facade.

When Kael dispelled the shadows, Marcus stood frozen, his bravado shattered. The mask of confidence slipped, revealing a genuine terror in his eyes. He attempted to regain composure, but the subtle tremor in his voice betrayed his unease.

"You think that's going to rattle me?" Marcus scoffed, but his attempt to sound defiant fell flat. A bead of sweat glistened on his forehead, and his eyes darted nervously around the room.

Reka exchanged a glance with Kael, acknowledging the shift in the dynamics. Once filled with boasts and rivalry, the locker room now held an undercurrent of tension. As they left for the Elemental Race and Combat, Reka couldn't shake the realization that the challenges ahead were destined to be more intricate and perilous than they had ever imagined.

~~~

After the intense practice battle in the Combat Arena, Reka, Kael, Aiden, and Zara walked back to their apartment, the echoes of their elemental clashes still lingering in the air. The
~~~

setting sun painted the sky with hues of orange and pink as they strolled through the Academy's courtyard, their minds buzzing with discussions about the day's practice and the upcoming Elemental Race and Combat.

Reka led the conversation, her excitement evident. "Did you see how Marcus tried to play it cool after our little locker room encounter? Classic. He won't admit it, but I think Kael's illusion got under his skin."

Kael shrugged, a smirk playing on his lips. "Just a taste of what's to come. We'll face challenges, not just in combat but in dealing with personalities like Marcus. Gotta be ready for everything."

Aiden chimed in, "Speaking of challenges, we should strategize. What if the race throws unexpected obstacles our way? We need a plan for each element – Earth, Wind, Digital, and Mind."

Zara, always the voice of optimism, added, "Let's focus on our strengths. Reka's agility, Kael's illusions, Aiden's water manipulation, and my energy manipulation. We can leverage each element strategically."

As they continued discussing strategies, the Academy's spires loomed in the distance, their apartment awaiting them. Kael emphasized the importance of teamwork, "We stick together, no matter what. The race is not just about winning but proving our unity."

Reka nodded in agreement, "Absolutely. And we need to be adaptive. What if the checkpoints have challenges related to each element? We should be ready to switch roles on the fly."

Always thinking ahead, Aiden added, "And let's not forget the combat aspect. Marcus and his team may have other tricks up their sleeves. We should be prepared for unexpected encounters."

~~~

As the friends reached their apartment, anticipation buzzed in the air. They found an ornate envelope waiting for them, the emblem of Iakrus Academy stamped on its surface. Reka eagerly opened it, revealing a detailed map with a path. Alongside the map was a message from the Grandmaster.

"Dear Students,

Enclosed is the map for the Elemental Race and Combat, provided earlier than tradition dictates, with hopes that your teams may better strategize and prepare for the formidable
~~~

challenges that lie ahead. In the twists and turns of our enchanted grounds, you will find the path to victory.

I extend my apologies for any disruption this deviation from tradition may cause. May your elemental mastery guide you to triumph and success in this unique endeavor. Embrace the challenges with resilience and unity.

Best regards,

Grandmaster Guadalupe"

Reka spread the map on the table, and the friends huddled around it. The map showcased the sprawling academy grounds, from the Whispering Grove to the Combat Arena, with marked checkpoints and potential challenges. As they traced the routes with their fingers, the room filled with a renewed sense of determination.

"We've got this," Reka declared, her eyes reflecting the map's intricacies. "Let's go through it and finalize our strategies. With the map, we can anticipate the challenges and plan accordingly."

V

<u>Chapter 5: The Race Of Elements</u>

The morning of the Elemental Race and Combat dawned with a vibrant energy, anticipation buzzing in the air like a tangible force. Reka, ever the mischief-maker, couldn't resist the opportunity to add a touch of tradition and magic to the occasion. With a mischievous smile playing on her lips, she reached into her satchel and pulled out a bundle of polished bamboo bracelets, each one intricately crafted with delicate patterns.

"Alright, everyone, gather around," Reka called out, her voice carrying a hint of excitement. Her friends gathered in a circle and turned their attention to her, curiosity gleaming in their eyes. "I've got something special for each of you."

As she distributed the bracelets, Reka's eyes sparkled with enthusiasm. "These are handmade bamboo bracelets, passed down through generations in our clan. They're more than just accessories; they're symbols of protection and good fortune. Wear them during the race, and may they bring you luck and strength."

Aiden, always appreciative of thoughtful gestures, admired the craftsmanship of his bracelet as he slipped it onto his wrist. "Thanks, Reka. This means a lot."

With the bracelets securely in place, Zara stepped forward, a small pouch clutched in her hand. "Now, it's my turn to contribute to our pre-race rituals." With a flourish, she opened the pouch, revealing a collection of shimmering time crystal shards, each one emitting a soft, ethereal glow.

"These are time crystal shards," Zara explained, her voice carrying a hint of reverence. "Rare and precious, they hold the power to grant glimpses into the past. They say that by reflecting on our journey and experiences, we can gain valuable insights to guide us forward."

As Aiden reached out to touch one of the shards, a sudden surge of energy coursed through him, sending a shiver down his spine. His surroundings blurred and shifted, and suddenly, he found himself standing in a grove surrounded by ancient trees. But instead of tranquility, he felt a queasy sensation in the pit of his stomach, as if something was amiss.

The air was thick with magic, but it felt heavy and oppressive, casting a shadow over the grove. Despite the beauty of the surroundings, an underlying sense of foreboding lingered in the air.

In the distance, he saw a stone adorned with glowing runes, each symbol pulsating with a faint, otherworldly light. As he gazed upon it, a sense of unease washed over him, like a warning echoing in his mind.

Before he could explore further, the vision took an unexpected turn. Suddenly, the grove transformed. The sky darkened, and the trees seemed to whisper secrets of ancient mysteries.

Aiden felt a chill run down his spine as he witnessed strange and unsettling imagery. Shadows danced around him, twisting and contorting into grotesque forms. The air crackled with an ominous energy, and the atmosphere grew heavy with dread.

In the midst of this surreal experience, Aiden's senses were overwhelmed by a cacophony of whispers, each voice carrying a cryptic message. The grove seemed to pulse with a sinister presence, and Aiden couldn't shake the feeling that he was being watched by unseen eyes.

Just as suddenly as it had begun, the vision ended, leaving Aiden disoriented and shaken. He stumbled back, trying to make sense of what he had just witnessed. Turning to his friends, he could only manage a shaky whisper.

"I... I don't know what that was, but it wasn't right. We need to be careful."

~~~

The locker room hummed with nervous energy as Reka, Aiden, Zara, and Kael made their final preparations for the impending race. The air was charged with anticipation, each member of the team silently going over their individual strategies and mentally steeling themselves for the challenge ahead.
~~~

Her hands were steady as she fastened her gear; Reka couldn't help but feel a surge of excitement mixed with a hint of nervousness. This race wasn't just about proving themselves against their peers; it was an opportunity to showcase their skills and unity as a team.

Aiden meticulously checked his weapons, ensuring that each one was in prime condition for the race. His movements were deliberate and focused, a testament to his years of training and dedication to honing his martial skills.

Zara, shining with determination, moved among her teammates, offering encouragement and support. Her unwavering optimism was like a beacon of light in the midst of their pre-race jitters, reminding them that they were in this together.

Ever the strategist, Kael paced back and forth, mentally mapping out the race course and envisioning various scenarios they might encounter along the way. His mind was a whirlwind of calculations and contingencies, ensuring they were prepared for whatever challenges awaited them.

As they gathered around in a huddle, their hands clasped together in a show of solidarity, a sense of camaraderie washed over them. They were a team, bound by a shared goal and a deep-rooted trust in each other's abilities.

With a final nod to one another, they straightened their postures, their expressions determined as they prepared to face whatever the race had in store for them.

They were ready.

~~~

The anticipation crackled in the air like static electricity as the competitors gathered at the starting line, a colorful array of teams from various elemental disciplines. Reka, Aiden, Zara, and Kael stood shoulder to shoulder, their faces set in determined expressions as they mentally prepared for the challenge ahead.

Amidst the throng of contestants, Marcus and his group loomed like dark clouds on the horizon. Their presence was palpable, a silent challenge hanging in the air as they exchanged smirks and taunts with Reka's team, their attempts to lower their confidence evident.

With his usual air of arrogance, Marcus leaned in close, his voice dripping with disdain. "You think you stand a chance,
~~~

misfits? This race is about skill and strategy, not flimsy bracelets and trinkets."

Reka, refusing to be rattled, met his gaze head-on, her eyes flashing with defiance. "We'll let our actions speak for us, Marcus. Just focus on keeping up."

Before Marcus could respond with another barb, the race official stepped forward, silencing the murmurs with a raised hand. His voice boomed across the gathering, commanding attention as he outlined the rules of the race.

"The use of elements is prohibited," he declared, his words echoing off the surrounding walls. "This race will test your martial skills and weapon proficiency, not your elemental mastery."

Aiden exchanged a glance with his teammates, a flicker of concern passing between them. While they were skilled in elemental manipulation, this race would require them to rely solely on their physical abilities and weaponry - a daunting prospect, but one they were determined to conquer.

The official continued, his tone grave as he outlined the consequences for breaking the rules. "Killing, crippling, and permanent injury are strictly prohibited. Any team found in violation will be expelled and punished accordingly. Your group will be disqualified from the race and combat for three years."

The gravity of the consequences hung heavy in the air, a sobering reminder of the stakes they faced. Reka's team exchanged solemn nods, a silent agreement to abide by the rules and uphold the integrity of the competition.

"And remember," the official concluded, his voice ringing out with authority, "only the first 15 groups will be selected for the combat. There are a total of 30 groups competing today. Now, let the race begin!"

VI

<u>Chapter 6: The Whispering Grove</u>

The starting signal echoed across the racecourse, a sharp crack that pierced through the tension-laden air, igniting a frenzy of movement among the assembled competitors. In the heart of the throng, Aiden's team stood poised, their determination etched upon their faces as they prepared to embark on the challenge that lay ahead.

Aiden, ever the embodiment of quick thinking and decisive action, wasted no time in seizing the initiative. He unleashed the Wind Lash Kick with a deft motion, a display of elemental mastery that conjured a barrier of swirling gusts. The tempestuous winds surged behind them, a formidable obstacle that threatened to thwart the progress of their nearest rivals, effectively slowing their advance and creating a buffer zone between them and the competition.

Meanwhile, Kael, the stalwart warrior of the group, surveyed their surroundings with a keen eye honed by years of battle-hardened experience. His gaze fell upon a dummy tree, a cleverly placed obstacle designed to impede the progress of any group that dared to stray from the designated path. With a fluid motion, he swung his battle axe, the blade biting deep into the wooden trunk with a satisfying crunch. The obstacle fell with a resounding thud, shattered by Kael's decisive stroke, clearing the way for Aiden's team to forge ahead unhindered.

Reka tapped into the depths of her formidable martial abilities as their rivals scrambled to overcome the unexpected challenges. With a focused intensity that bordered on the sublime, she channeled her energy into a Portal Punch, a technique honed through years of disciplined training and unwavering dedication to her craft.

In an instant, shadows coalesced around her, weaving a swirling vortex that enveloped her form in its inky embrace. With a graceful leap, Reka vanished into the darkness, her figure disappearing from sight as she traversed through the ephemeral portal, leaving behind naught but a faint shimmer of energy in her wake.

Time seemed to warp and bend as Aiden, Kael, Reka, and Zara journeyed through the shadow realm, the ethereal landscape passing in a blur around her. She emerged from the depths of the shadowy abyss in mere moments, her form materializing with a silent grace at a distant point along the racecourse.

The sudden displacement left their adversaries stunned, their expressions a mixture of disbelief and awe as they struggled to comprehend how Aiden's team had surged so far ahead in such a short span of time.

~~~

The starting signal reverberated across the racecourse, and Marcus gritted his teeth as Aiden's team surged ahead. His eyes narrowed as he watched Aiden execute a Wind Lash Kick, creating a barrier of swirling winds that obstructed their competitors. Frustration churned in Marcus's gut as his own team struggled to navigate through the gusts.

Kael's swift action didn't escape Marcus's notice. With a decisive swing of his battle axe, Kael effortlessly cleaved through
~~~

a dummy tree blocking their path. Marcus cursed under his breath, recognizing the tactical advantage gained by Aiden's group.

But it was Reka's sudden disappearance that left Marcus seething with jealousy and admiration. He watched in disbelief as she executed a Portal Punch, disappearing into a shadowy vortex and reappearing far ahead of the pack. The audacity of their maneuver ignited a fire in Marcus's chest, fueling his determination to catch up.

As Aiden's team pulled ahead, Marcus's mind raced with frustration and envy. How could they have gained such a lead so quickly? The unexpected display of skill and coordination from his rivals threatened to shatter his confidence, but Marcus refused to yield.

With a fierce glint in his eyes, Marcus rallied his team, his resolve hardened by the challenge before them. They might have fallen behind at the start, but Marcus vowed to reclaim their position and prove their superiority.

The Elemental Race was far from over, and Marcus was determined to show Aiden's team that they weren't the only ones capable of seizing victory. He led his team forward with grit and determination, determined to overcome every obstacle in their path and emerge triumphant.

<div style="text-align:center">~~~</div>

Aiden felt a surge of exhilaration as his team maintained their lead, surging forward with determination and purpose. With each stride, he felt the weight of their collective effort, propelling them closer to victory. Yet, amidst the intensity of the race, a nagging thought tugged at the edges of his consciousness—the Whispering Grove.

The whispers of legends and folklore had always intrigued Aiden, and now, with the race unfolding around them, the allure of the mysterious grove beckoned. He glanced at his teammates, each focused on the path ahead, their determination palpable. But Aiden couldn't shake the feeling that venturing into the Whispering Grove could hold the key to unlocking a deeper understanding of their journey.

Aiden's mind wandered as they continued their rapid pace through the rugged terrain, imagining the secrets that awaited within the ancient grove. Legends spoke of mystical energies and forgotten wisdom hidden amidst the whispering leaves, a sanctuary untouched by the passage of time.

With a silent resolve, Aiden made a decision. He turned to his teammates, his voice cutting through the rush of wind and their footsteps pounding. "Guys, I know we're leading the race, but I think we should make a detour. The Whispering Grove is nearby, and I have a feeling there might be something important there."

His teammates exchanged glances, their expressions a mix of curiosity and determination. Reka nodded, her eyes sparkling with intrigue. "I'm with you, Aiden. If there's a chance to uncover something valuable, we should take it."

Kael grinned, his enthusiasm evident. "Sounds like an adventure. Lead the way, Aiden."

With their decision made, Aiden veered off the main path, leading his team toward the elusive Whispering Grove. As they ventured deeper into the wilderness, the air seemed to hum with anticipation, the whispers of the grove growing louder with each step.

Ahead, the ancient trees loomed like silent sentinels, their gnarled branches reaching toward the sky. Aiden's heart quickened with anticipation as they entered the grove, the atmosphere thick with a sense of ancient magic and untold secrets.

A sudden creak echoed through the grove, startling Aiden. His instincts kicked in, and he glanced down, only to realize that he had unwittingly stepped on a pressure plate of some sort.

Aiden glanced up at his friends, and a scared expression flashed for a second before being replaced with a playful one. "Umm, guys, Did I just step on the wrong stone, or did I accidentally activate something that's gonna make this day a lot more interesting?"

Then, with a deafening roar, the grove erupted into a blinding explosion of vibrant light, engulfing everything in its path.

~~~

With a swift and decisive swing of his sword, Marcus unleashed a ferocious blow, the metallic clang of his blade meeting resistance echoing through the air. The creature before them let out a guttural roar as blood spilled crimson upon the ground, marking the end of their arduous battle. As the beast collapsed, its life force extinguished, Marcus and his team stood amidst the aftermath, their faces stained with sweat and grime.

Amidst the victory, Alex, the tech master of Marcus's team, spoke up, his voice tinged with urgency. "Marcus, I believe we've
~~~

overtaken Aiden's team. My scanaroid indicates no humanoid signatures in the vicinity."

Marcus's gaze hardened as he turned to face Alex, his grip tightening around the tech master's throat. With a fierce glare, he demanded answers, suspicion dripping from every word. "You're the one who guided us here, Alex. Are you working for our team, or are you leading us into danger to aid the Water-Boy and his team of freaks?"

Caught off guard and struggling for breath, Alex's response was strained. "I-I'm sorry, Marcus. It was an oversight, I swear."

Marcus released his grip with a dismissive snarl, sending Alex crashing to the forest floor. Dusting himself off with an air of indignation, Marcus's resolve hardened. "I don't care about being in the top 15. What matters is crushing those misfits under our heel."

As Marcus and his team prepared to forge ahead, a sudden burst of blinding light enveloped them, casting their surroundings in an ethereal glow.

~~~

As the radiant light faded, Kael's voice cut through the silence, its tone tinged with a mix of exasperation and concern.
~~~

"Aiden, if you pull a stunt like that again, I swear I'll turn you into a cockroach."

Aiden chuckled weakly, his voice barely audible amidst the eerie quiet of the grove. "No need for that threat, Kael. It seems the gods have already issued their punishment. I've been temporarily robbed of my sight."

Kael's expression softened, the concern in his eyes mirroring the unease that settled over them all. "Wait, what? You too?"

Reka and Zara's voices joined in unison, a harmony of disbelief that seemed to resonate through the stillness around them. "Wait, we thought that was only us..."

As they ventured deeper into the grove, a sense of foreboding seemed to cling to the air like a heavy mist. The ancient trees loomed overhead, their twisted branches casting long, shifting shadows that danced eerily across the forest floor. The silence was oppressive, broken only by the soft rustle of leaves and the occasional creak of branches swaying in the breeze.

Reka exchanged a worried glance with Kael and Zara, their unspoken fears palpable in the air between them. It was as if the grove itself held its breath, as though anticipating some monumental event that hovered just beyond the edge of their perception.

Their footsteps echoed softly against the earth as they finally reached the heart of the grove. The air crackled with an electric tension, every sound amplified to an almost deafening degree. The ground beneath their feet trembled, sending shivers of unease coursing through their bodies.

Then, a stone erupted from the earth before them as if responding to some unseen command. Its surface was etched with intricate glyphs that pulsed with an ethereal radiance, casting a mesmerizing glow over the surrounding foliage. Aiden's heart skipped a beat as he beheld the symbols; his mind suddenly plunged into a whirlwind of memories and sensations.

In an instant, the world around him dissolved into a kaleidoscope of images and emotions, each one more vivid and disorienting than the last. It was as if the stone itself had become a gateway to another realm, pulling him inexorably into its depths.

The glyphs danced before his eyes, their movements fluid and hypnotic, weaving a tapestry of ancient knowledge and forgotten truths. Aiden's head throbbed with a dull ache, each pulse sending shockwaves of pain through his skull.

For a moment that stretched on into eternity, he was lost in the swirling maelstrom of his own mind, adrift in a sea of fragmented memories and half-formed thoughts. And then, just as suddenly as it had begun, the onslaught ceased, leaving him gasping for breath and struggling to make sense of the world around him.

Aiden's voice emerged from the haze of his disorientation, filled with a mixture of wonder and confusion. "Guys, I don't know what language that is, but... I can understand all of it."

As Aiden confessed his unsettling ability to comprehend the enigmatic language of the stone, his friends exchanged wary glances, grappling with the implications of his revelation. Reka's brows furrowed in concentration as she stepped closer to the stone, her gaze fixed on its shimmering surface.

"You can understand it? What does it say?" Reka inquired, her voice laced with a mixture of fascination and concern.

Aiden hesitated, his mind still reeling from the jarring experience. "I'm not sure... It's like... It's like the words are speaking directly to my mind, bypassing my ears altogether."

Zara's eyes widened with realization as she approached, her gaze fixated on the ancient glyphs. "This... This is a long-lost text of the Primordials, the ancient gods. Few possess the knowledge to decipher it, and those who do are millennia old."

Aiden's expression darkened with realization. "This was a bad idea. We need to get out of here, now."

As they turned to leave the grove, a deep, resonant voice reverberated from the skies above, freezing them in their tracks.

"The crystals four, with power untold,"

VII

CHAPTER 7: THE PROPHECY OF ELEMENTS

"The crystals four, with power untold,

Scattered wide, in lands of old.

Water, Fire, Time, and Dark,

Guardians of each, their mark.

Through trials dire, they must be found,

Their essence pure, unbound.

For in their union, lies the key,

To banish evil, and set free.

Water's flow, Fire's blaze,

Time's wisdom, Dark's embrace.

Together forged, a force so bright,

To vanquish shadows, and restore the light.

But heed this warning, lest we fall,

For darkness waits, to claim us all.

With crystals four, our hope shall rise,

And in their glow, evil dies."

The voice echoed through the grove, leaving a profound silence in its wake. Aiden and his friends stood motionless, the weight of the prophecy settling over them like a shroud. They exchanged glances, their faces etched with a mixture of awe and trepidation.

Aiden was the first to break the silence, his voice barely a whisper. "The elements in the prophecy... they're ours. Water, Fire, Time, and Darkness. That's... that's creepy."

Reka's eyes widened, and she shivered involuntarily. "It's like the prophecy is about us. We have to get out of here. Now."

Zara nodded vigorously, her usually calm demeanor shaken. "Let's move. This place is giving me the creeps."

With a sense of urgency, they turned and hastened their steps, eager to leave behind the grove and its eerie prophecies. The words continued to echo in their minds, a constant reminder of the path that lay ahead and the destiny they could not escape. As they emerged from the grove, the oppressive atmosphere lifted, but the sense of foreboding lingered, urging them onward to fulfill their daunting quest.

~~~

As the radiant light dissipated, Marcus and his team found themselves plunged into a state of disorientation. The sudden transition from blinding brightness to the dimly lit grove left them momentarily bewildered, their senses struggling to adjust to the shifting surroundings.

Amidst the lingering haze of confusion, they pressed onward, their movements slow and tentative as they navigated the winding pathways of the grove. The air was heavy with anticipation, each step forward fraught with uncertainty.

After what felt like an eternity of navigating the twisting paths, they emerged from the depths of the grove, greeted by the sight of a yawning canyon stretching out before them. The
~~~

chasm yawned wide, its depths shrouded in an impenetrable darkness that seemed to swallow the feeble light.

Marcus squinted into the distance, his gaze fixed on the precarious bridge that spanned the gaping expanse. The bridge appeared fragile and unstable, its weathered planks groaning under the weight of time and neglect.

A sense of unease settled over the group as they surveyed the treacherous path ahead, each member exchanging wary glances as they contemplated the perilous journey that lay before them. Yet, despite the palpable sense of danger, there was a steely determination in their eyes, a silent acknowledgment of the challenges they faced and the necessity of pressing onward.

With a collective breath, Marcus and his team steeled themselves for the daunting task ahead, their resolve unyielding as they prepared to brave the treacherous crossing that stood between them and their destination. Without hesitation, they moved forward, their footsteps echoing in the canyon's depths as they approached the narrow bridge. Just as they were about to take their first step, a voice rang out from across the chasm. "HIYA!" Aiden's group swung into view, their presence both surprising and welcome.

"Did we crash the party, Marcus?"

Marcus's initial shock quickly turned to a mix of irritation and suspicion. "Of course you did, Aiden. Always showing up at the most unexpected times," he retorted, his eyes narrowing as he gauged the newcomers.

Reka, Zara, and Kael landed beside Aiden, each exuding confidence and readiness. Reka glanced at the bridge and then back at Marcus's team. "Seems like we've both got the same daunting task ahead of us," she observed, her tone serious.

Zara stepped forward, her keen eyes scanning the canyon and the bridge. "Safety in numbers, maybe? We should figure out the best way to cross," she suggested, her practical mind already formulating a plan.

Kael nodded in agreement. "We need to cross safely and steadily. Let's not rush and make sure the bridge can hold us."

Before they could finalize a plan, other teams began arriving, their presence adding to the tension. The bridge was the only way across, and everyone was clearly anxious to get to the other side first.

Kael raised his voice to address the gathered groups. "Alright, everyone. We need to cross safely and steadily. One team at a time. Let's not rush and make sure the bridge can hold us."

The teams nodded in agreement, tension evident but a sense of order prevailing. They began to cross one by one, each team moving cautiously, aware of the bridge's fragility.

Marcus and his team waited, their eyes never leaving the other teams. As Aiden's group stepped onto the bridge, Marcus's eyes narrowed. They moved with caution, and their progress was slow but steady. The bridge creaked and swayed under their weight, but it held.

As Aiden's group neared the middle of the bridge, Marcus exchanged a glance with his team. They made a break for the bridge without warning, sprinting across with reckless abandon. The sudden rush of movement sent shockwaves through the already unstable structure.

"Hey, what are you doing?" Aiden shouted, realizing too late the danger they were in.

The bridge groaned and began to give way. Planks splintered, and ropes snapped under the combined weight and frantic motion. The teams already on the bridge scrambled to hold on, panic setting in.

The bridge collapsed with a final, resounding crack, sending everyone plunging into the darkness below.

VIII

CHAPTER 8: ELEMENT AWAKENING

Aiden woke to the sensation of cold water splashing against his face. He sputtered and blinked rapidly, trying to clear the confusion from his mind. As his vision sharpened, he saw Kael, Reka, and Zara standing over him, relief evident on their faces.

"You're awake!" Reka exclaimed, her voice tinged with a mixture of concern and joy.

Kael offered a wry smile, lowering his hand from the makeshift water bucket they had used to rouse him. "Had to make sure you didn't leave us again, you know."

Zara knelt beside him, her eyes scanning his face for any signs of injury. "How do you feel, Aiden? Can you remember what happened?"

Aiden sat up slowly, groaning as his muscles protested the movement. His mind was a blur of fractured memories and intense sensations. "The bridge... I remember it collapsing. We were falling. Then... nothing."

Kael exchanged a glance with Reka and Zara before speaking. "It was more than just a fall, Aiden. Somehow, you transported us back in time, just before Marcus's team made their move. You used your water powers to create a barrier and stop them."

Aiden's eyes widened in disbelief. "I did what? But my element is water. How can I control time?"

Zara nodded, her expression serious. "Yes, it did. But you used water from the stream below to cushion our fall. You saved everyone, Aiden. Without you, it could have been a lot worse."

Aiden took a moment to process their words. He looked around, seeing the other teams scattered around, checking each other for injuries and gathering their bearings. Everyone seemed to be okay, thanks to his quick thinking.

"I... I don't know how I did it," he admitted, still trying to wrap his head around the enormity of what had happened. "It's like my instincts took over."

Reka placed a reassuring hand on his shoulder. "Whatever it was, you saved us. That's what matters."

Kael offered a hand to help Aiden stand. "We need to figure out our next move. Marcus's team might still be out there, and we can't afford to be caught off guard again."

Aiden accepted Kael's hand, rising to his feet with renewed determination. "You're right. We have to keep moving. We can't let them get ahead of us."

As they regrouped, Zara pointed towards a narrow path leading out of the canyon. "There's a way up. It looks steep, but it's our best bet."

~~~

Looking at the broken bridge in front of them, Marcus was stumped. How did Aiden know what he was going to do? He turned to Alex and said, "Build us a bridge to get out of here."
~~~

Alex, nodding his head, got to work. About fifteen minutes later, the bridge and Marcus were ready to win. Together, they crossed the bridge. After crossing, they were jubilant, celebrating their apparent victory.

Then they saw Aiden and all the other teams climbing up the chasm.

Marcus's eyes widened in disbelief as Aiden and his group emerged from the depths, determination etched on their faces. The other teams, bruised and battered, followed close behind, their expressions a mix of relief and resolve.

"We need to move quickly," Marcus said, urgency in his voice. "Alex, activate the jet packs."

Alex nodded, quickly activating the team's emergency jet packs. With a burst of energy, they lifted off the ground, soaring into the air and gaining a significant lead. The jet packs hummed with power, propelling them forward at a rapid pace. The ground below became a blur as they soared over the landscape, their lead extending with every second.

Just as they were celebrating their escape and the lead they had gained, a sharp whip of water lashed out from below. Aiden, his eyes fierce with determination, had conjured a water whip and struck them down with precision. The force of the water whip was immense, and Marcus and his team were sent flying, their jet packs sputtering as they crashed to the ground ahead of the canyon.

The impact was jarring, and they tumbled across the rough terrain before coming to a halt. The wind was knocked out of them, and they scrambled to regain their footing. The realization that they had lost their advantage hit them hard.

Kael turned to Aiden, urgency in his voice. "We don't have much time. We have to get to the finish line."

Aiden nodded, understanding the gravity of their situation. He looked around at the other teams, who were also recovering from the fall. "Let's move. Everyone, come quickly!"

Together, Aiden, Kael, Reka, and Zara rallied the remaining groups. The other teams, shaken but inspired by Aiden's swift action, followed their lead. They moved swiftly with determination and newfound unity, navigating the treacherous terrain with a singular focus. The path ahead was fraught with danger, but with their combined strength and resolve, they pushed forward, their sights set firmly on their goal.

The finish line awaited, and they would not be deterred. The landscape was unforgiving, with jagged rocks and steep inclines, but they pressed on, their collective will driving them forward.

The sun was beginning to set, casting long shadows over the terrain, but the dimming light only served to sharpen their resolve.

As they moved, they communicated wordlessly, their actions coordinated by instinct and trust. Aiden led the way, his water abilities smoothing the path and providing a measure of safety where the ground was unstable. With his mastery of darkness, Kael shrouded their movements, making it harder for any potential threats to pinpoint their location. Reka and Zara brought up the rear, their vigilance ensuring that no one was left behind.

The race was on, and every second counted. The urgency of their mission spurred them on, and despite the exhaustion that gnawed at their limbs, they kept moving. The finish line was within reach, and they would not let anything stand in their way.

IX

CHAPTER 9: THE FINAL STRETCH

The final stretch of their arduous journey lay before them. The sun had dipped below the horizon, casting a twilight glow that bathed the landscape in shades of orange and purple. The finish line, marked by a towering arch adorned with ancient runes, stood just ahead.

Aiden's group moved with urgency, their breaths coming in short, determined bursts. They could hear the sounds of other teams closing in behind them, the collective resolve palpable in the air. Every group member felt the weight of the moment;

their journey had been long and fraught with peril, but the end was finally in sight.

"Keep pushing!" Aiden urged his voice, a rallying cry that spurred them onward.

Kael, Reka, and Zara ran alongside him, their expressions focused and fierce. The finish line was just a few hundred yards away, and they poured every ounce of their remaining energy into closing the distance.

From behind, Marcus's group emerged, still determined despite their recent setback. Marcus's eyes were fixed on the finish line, his jaw set with grim determination. Having recovered from the water whip attack, Alex moved with surprising speed, his digital constructs assisting their advance.

The two groups raced neck and neck, the ground beneath them a blur of dust and determination. Equally exhausted but driven by the desire to complete their quest, other teams followed closely behind, their collective will driving them toward the goal.

Aiden glanced to his side and saw Marcus gaining ground. He felt a surge of competitive spirit but knew this was about more than winning. It was about proving their worth, about fulfilling the destiny that had been thrust upon them.

"Don't let up!" Kael shouted, urging his teammates to push harder.

With a final burst of speed, Aiden and his team reached the towering arch. Little did they know that Marcus' team was catching up to them.

Just as they crossed the finish line, Marcus's team was right on their heels. The ancient runes on the arch began to glow brighter, reacting to the presence of the finishing teams. The ground beneath them trembled slightly as if acknowledging the completion of their quest.

Aiden's team stumbled to a halt, gasping for breath but filled with a sense of triumph. Marcus's team crossed just seconds later, their expressions a mixture of frustration and begrudging respect. The other teams arrived shortly after, collapsing in exhausted heaps, their faces reflecting relief and accomplishment.

Reka looked around, taking in the sight of the other competitors. "We did it," she said, her voice filled with both exhaustion and pride.

Zara nodded, her eyes scanning the horizon. "This is just the beginning. There's still so much to do."

Kael placed a reassuring hand on Aiden's shoulder. "We proved ourselves today. We can face whatever comes next."

Marcus approached Aiden, his eyes filled with hostility. "Enjoy this while it lasts, Aiden. This isn't over, not by a long shot," he spat, his tone laced with venom.

Aiden met his glare with a calm, unwavering gaze. "We're ready for whatever comes next, Marcus."

Marcus sneered and turned away, his team following closely behind. The rivalry between them was far from resolved, the animosity still simmering beneath the surface.

As the sun set completely, the twilight giving way to night, the first stars began to appear in the sky. The competitors gathered around the arch, a sense of camaraderie beginning to form among some despite the clear tensions. They had all endured countless challenges to reach this point, and in that shared experience, they found a new strength.

The future of Ipesia was still uncertain, and the prophecy loomed over them like a shadow. But there was a spark of hope in that moment of collective victory. They had shown their strength, their resilience, and their unity. And with those qualities, they knew they could face any challenge that lay ahead.

As they stood together at the finish line, the path ahead seemed a little brighter, illuminated by their shared determination and newfound camaraderie. The journey was far from over, but for now, they could take solace in the fact that they had overcome the odds and emerged victorious.

And with that, their eyes turned to the horizon, ready to face whatever new adventures awaited them in the realm of Ipesia.

~~~ THE START OF THE END ~~~

Epilogue

In the distant region of Ipesia known as Alcyron Peaks, a desolate landscape stretched as far as the eye could see. Jagged rock formations and sparse vegetation marked the terrain, creating an otherworldly panorama. At the heart of this barren land lay an ancient cavern, its entrance hidden amidst the rugged rocks. Deep within, the air was cool and damp, carrying a scent of earth and forgotten secrets.

A lone figure treaded cautiously through the dimly lit cavern, his footsteps echoing off the walls. His name was Loran, a master weapon maker known throughout Ipesia for crafting legendary tools of war. His reputation was built on a foundation of skill, craftsmanship, and the creation of weapons that had turned the tide of battles. Today, he had journeyed to the heart of Alcyron Peaks in search of the fabled Aquarite, a rare ore said to possess the essence of water itself. This unique material was rumored to bestow incredible power upon weapons and artifacts, a temptation too great for Loran to resist.

Loran's lantern cast flickering shadows as he ventured deeper into the heart of the cave. His eyes, accustomed to the dim light, scanned the walls, seeking the telltale glimmer of Aquarite. He knew that this ore could reshape the balance of power across Ipesia. The weapon he would forge with it could change the course of history, tipping the scales in favor of those who possessed it.

The rhythmic water drip echoed through the cavern, and the air grew heavier as Loran's anticipation heightened. He had heard whispers of treacherous traps and formidable guardians, but his determination drove him forward. The cavern walls seemed to close in around him, bearing witness to his unwavering purpose.

As he navigated the labyrinthine passages, Loran's senses suddenly heightened. A sense of foreboding settled upon him like a heavy shroud. He glanced upward and noticed a peculiar change in the air—dark, swirling clouds gathered in the chamber's ceiling, blotting out any trace of the sky beyond.

The clouds began to descend, tendrils of darkness snaking downward with an unnatural purpose. Loran's heart raced as he realized the clouds were more than just a meteorological anomaly. Fear seized him, and he fumbled to draw his weapon— a finely crafted blade, an extension of his very soul.

A chilling voice reverberated through the chamber, both ethereal and menacing. "Haha, my plan is set into motion," it hissed, words echoing off the walls in an unsettling chorus.

Loran's grip tightened around his weapon, his knuckles white. He gritted his teeth and faced the descending darkness. "Who's there? Show yourself!" he demanded, his voice trembling.

The voice laughed, a sound that seemed to come from all directions. "You seek power, Loran. But power has its price."

The shadows surged forward in an instant, coalescing into a malevolent form. Loran's blade met the shadows in a desperate clash, but his strikes passed through the form as if it were smoke. The darkness engulfed him, and his world plunged into oblivion.

Unseen by any, the cavern returned to its silent stillness as if untouched by the turmoil that had unfolded within its depths. The ominous clouds retreated, leaving no trace of the struggle that had taken place.

Loran's vision cleared, and he found himself in a void of darkness, a realm between the worlds he knew. The mysterious voice echoed once more, its tone mocking and cruel. "You sought the Aquarite, Loran. You sought power. Now, you shall become an instrument of my design."

Loran struggled against the weight of the darkness, his mind a whirlwind of fear and confusion. "No, I won't be a pawn in your game!"

Laughter echoed around him, and he felt a searing pain lance through his being. Memories of his past, moments of triumph and loss, surged to the forefront of his mind. His essence was being unraveled, rewritten by the malevolent force that had ensnared him.

In the physical realm, Loran's body fell to the cavern floor, lifeless and void of the spark that once animated it. The darkness receded, leaving behind a sense of eerie tranquility. The cavern itself seemed to exhale, its walls sighing as if bearing witness to a profound shift in the world's balance.

Unknown to all, the clouds dispersed from the chamber's ceiling, merging with the shadows to become an indistinct haze that blended with the natural darkness of the cave.

Having achieved its sinister purpose, the ominous presence receded from this world, leaving nothing but a trail of uncertainty and fear in its wake.

<u>AFTERWORD</u>

Reading a lot is key to becoming a good writer. When you read a lot, writing comes more easily. Writing isn't just about putting words on paper; it's a way to explore different worlds and experiences. It lets adults see things from a child's perspective again. Starting to write is the first step towards achieving excellence. The process of writing a book sharpens your skills and nurtures your creativity.

Some studies suggest that creativity fades as we age, but creativity is always about taking risks. Children's literature falls into two categories: stories written by children and stories written for children. Literature created by children is more spontaneous and pure, helping adults reconnect with a child's mindset.

A Greek philosopher once said that humanity is at its best when children play. Children's literature is like play—it's a joyful and important form of expression. Within this genre, fantasy writing stands out as something special. Fantasy allows us to create entire worlds from scratch, making it different from other types of writing. It stretches the imagination and shows just how powerful our creativity can be.

Dr. Jonathan Long

Head of Academy

The Aga Khan Academy, Hyderabad

I would like to express my deepest gratitude to those who have supported and guided me throughout the creation of this novel.

To my parents, whose unwavering love and encouragement have been my foundation. Your belief in me has been the driving force behind my journey as a writer. Thank you for always being there and for inspiring me to chase my dreams.

To my mentors, Ms. Nivedita and Ms. Rema, your wisdom and guidance have been invaluable. Your insights and support have helped shape my writing and have been instrumental in bringing this story to life. Thank you for your patience, advice, and for believing in my potential.

To Dr. Neelam Himthani, whose incredible talent brought the cover of this book to life. Your artistic vision has captured the essence of my story beautifully. Thank you for your dedication and for creating a cover that perfectly represents "The Chronicles of Ipesia."

To Mr. Ravi Tiwari, for your meticulous editing and formatting. Your attention to detail and commitment to excellence have ensured that this book is polished and ready for the world. Thank you for your hard work and for helping to make this book the best it can be.

Finally, to all the readers who have embarked on this journey with me, thank you. Your support means the world to me, and I hope you have found joy and adventure within these pages.

Disclaimer

This book is a work of fiction. Names, characters, places, and incidents either are products of the author's imagination or are used fictitiously. Any resemblance to actual events, locales, or persons, living or dead, is entirely coincidental.

The views and opinions expressed in this book are those of the characters and do not necessarily reflect the official policy or position of any entity or individual. This book is intended for entertainment purposes only and is not meant to provide any form of advice or guidance.

About the Author

Yashvin is a talented young author from Hyderabad, India. At just 12 years old, Yashvin has already embarked on the exciting journey of storytelling with the creation of "The Chronicles of Ipesia: The Elemental Prophecy." Living with their parents and siblings, Yashvin finds inspiration in the world around them.

A lover of reading and writing, Yashvin spends countless hours immersed in books and creating captivating tales of their own. When not lost in the world of words, Yashvin enjoys playing with Legos, letting their imagination run wild to build fantastic creations.

Yashvin's passion for storytelling and their vibrant imagination promise many more adventures to come in the world of Ipesia and beyond.

At the outset, I want to give you a big thanks for reading this book. You could have chosen any other book, but you took mine, and I appreciate this. I hope you have at least a few actionable insights that will positively impact your daily life.

Can I ask for 30 seconds more of your time?

I'd love it if you could leave a review of the book. That will help me grow my readership by encouraging folks to take a chance on my books.

Keeping it straight - reviews are the lifeblood of any author.

It will take less than a minute of your time but will tremendously help me reach out to more people. Kindly provide your review at the store you bought this book from. And I'd love to see your review. Thanks for your support.